Sleeping with GHOSTS™

THE HOTEL AVIRA HAUNTINGS

CREATOR, WRITER,
GRAPHIC NOVEL COVER ARTIST
DAMIAN S SIMANKOWICZ

ARTIST
MARCELO SALAZA

COLORIST
MIKE STEFAN

LETTERER
PRIMAL ARCHETYPE

COVER ARTIST (ISSUES 1-3)
MAX MODA

SERIES LOGO DESIGNER
SARAH SIMANKOWICZ

PROJECT COORDINATOR
JASON DUBE

SPECIAL THANKS TO
Sally-Anne Simankowicz, Pat Gould, Patsy Gould,
and Scattered Studios, whose services made the
creation of this book possible.

facebook.com/damianssimankowiczart
instagram.com/damianssimankowicz

ISBN-13: 978-0-9942549-4-8

Sleeping with Ghosts

THE HOTEL AVIRA HAUNTINGS

CHAPTER 1: SEBASTIAN

AUSTRALIA. NEAR THE NEW SOUTH WALES BORDER TO MELBOURNE.
THE HOTEL AVIRA.
This is it, man.
End of the line.
RECEPTION.
If this place doesn't have something supernatural, nowhere will.

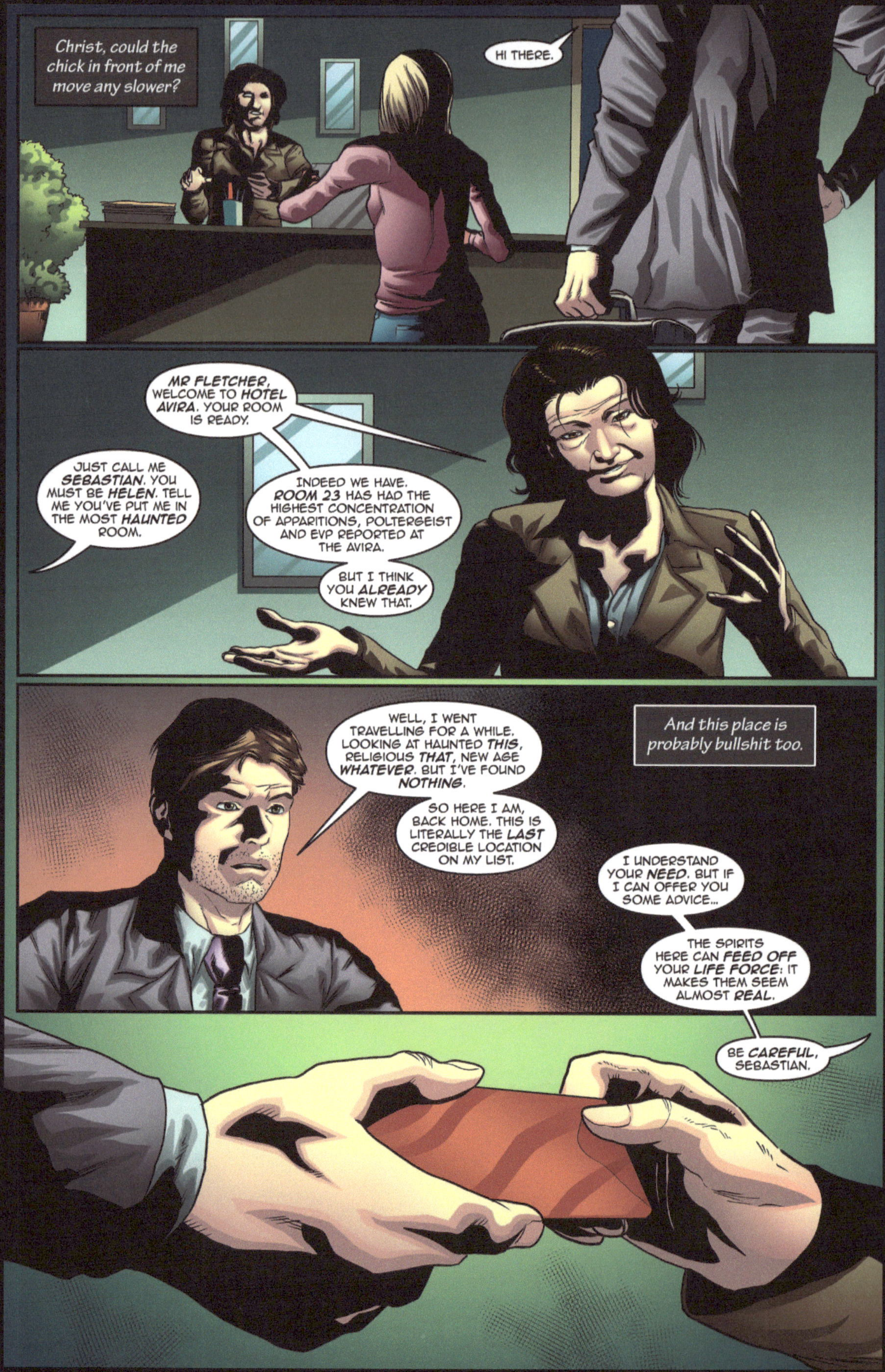

Christ, could the chick in front of me move any slower?
HI THERE.
MR FLETCHER, WELCOME TO HOTEL AVIRA. YOUR ROOM IS READY.
JUST CALL ME SEBASTIAN. YOU MUST BE HELEN. TELL ME YOU'VE PUT ME IN THE MOST HAUNTED ROOM.
INDEED WE HAVE. ROOM 23 HAS HAD THE HIGHEST CONCENTRATION OF APPARITIONS, POLTERGEIST AND EVP REPORTED AT THE AVIRA.
BUT I THINK YOU ALREADY KNEW THAT.
WELL, I WENT TRAVELLING FOR A WHILE. LOOKING AT HAUNTED THIS, RELIGIOUS THAT, NEW AGE WHATEVER. BUT I'VE FOUND NOTHING.
SO HERE I AM, BACK HOME. THIS IS LITERALLY THE LAST CREDIBLE LOCATION ON MY LIST.
And this place is probably bullshit too.
I UNDERSTAND YOUR NEED. BUT IF I CAN OFFER YOU SOME ADVICE...
THE SPIRITS HERE CAN FEED OFF YOUR LIFE FORCE: IT MAKES THEM SEEM ALMOST REAL.
BE CAREFUL, SEBASTIAN.

Nice sales pitch.

I haven't touched the button yet.
Is that a motion sensor?
PING

Where's the lift?

WHOA!
FOOM

PING

NICE TRICK. I SAID GHOSTS, NOT GIMMICKS.

THE SECOND FLOOR.
...AFTERNOON.
The infamous room twenty-three.
I knew it would be bullshit.
I'm so sick of this.
Have I had enough?
Yeah, I've had enough.
Did something just move past me?

Is that... ?
OH SHIT... THAT WAS REAL.
OH MY GOD. THAT WAS REAL!

This is where the old woman went.

HELLO? ANYONE THERE?

SECOND FLOOR CORRIDOR.
HELLO?

NOPE, JUST ME TALKING TO MYSELF.

What's going on with the lights?

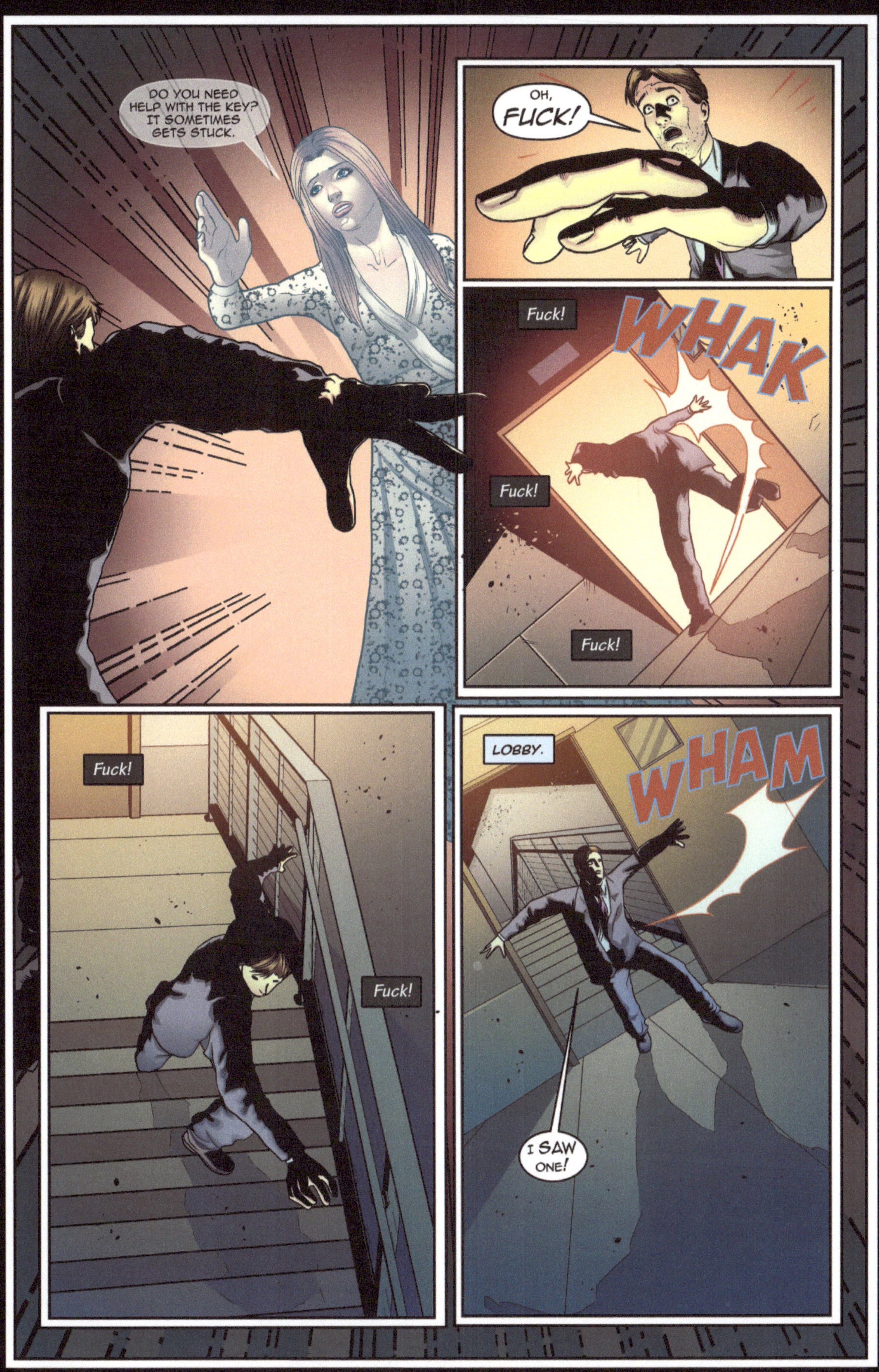

DO YOU NEED HELP WITH THE KEY? IT SOMETIMES GETS STUCK.
OH, FUCK!
Fuck!
WHAK
Fuck!
Fuck!

Fuck!
Fuck!

LOBBY.
WHAM
I SAW ONE!

I JUST SAW ONE! WELL, TWO ACTUALLY.
AH... AN ELDERLY MOTHER AND AN ADULT DAUGHTER, I THINK.
THAT WOULD BE CLAIRE AND HER MOTHER, THEY'RE HARMLESS.
THOUGH CLAIRE CAN BE QUITE ACTIVE.
IF YOU'D TOLD ME TEN MINUTES AGO THAT WOULD HAPPEN, I WOULDN'T HAVE BELIEVED IT.
IF YOU LIKE, I COULD MOVE YOU TO A DIFFERENT FLOOR? ONE WITH LESS ACTIVITY?
NO. NO, I'LL STAY ON THE SECOND FLOOR. THIS IS WHAT I CAME FOR.
HAHA, I'VE GOT GOOSE BUMPS!

IT'S HER!
SHE RARELY COMES DOWN THIS FAR.
CAN SHE SEE ME?
IT APPEARS CLAIRE IS CURIOUS ABOUT YOU, SEBASTIAN.
DO I KNOW YOU? YOU SEEM VERY FAMILIAR.
YES. YOU WERE GOING TO HELP ME WITH MY ROOM KEY, ON THE SECOND FLOOR?
SHALL WE?
WHAT SHOULD I DO?
THIS IS WHAT YOU CAME HERE FOR.

HI, I'M SEBASTIAN. YOU'RE CLAIRE, RIGHT?

YES. THE CUT OF YOUR SUIT IS STRANGE.
AH... HOW LONG HAVE YOU BEEN HERE?

NOT LONG.
Can she smell my cologne?

Did she just.. touch me?!

THE SECOND FLOOR.
AH, LADIES FIRST.
Why is she vanishing?
CLAIRE? WHERE'D YOU GO?
LOBBY LIFTS
CLAIRE?
She's gotta be here somewhere!
OUTSIDE THE HOTEL AVIRA.
What the.. ?
AH.. HELLO?

Man, this place just gets weirder and weirder.
RECEPTION.
I WAS JUST WITH CLAIRE, AND SHE VANISHED!
I'M NOT SURPRISED. MOST OF THE GHOSTS HERE DON'T REALISE THEY'RE DEAD.
AND THEY DON'T SEEM TO EXPERIENCE TIME THE WAY WE DO.
THEY CAN ACT VERY ODD.
YOU'RE NOT KIDDING.
ONE MOMENT, SEBASTIAN.
I HAVE TO GO SOMEWHERE.
UNPACK AND RELAX, WE'LL TALK MORE SOON.

GUEST ROOM.
SO UGLY...

AND HERE COMES THE FEVER.
YOU'LL DO IT AGAIN.

W-WHO SAID THAT?
YOU'LL ALWAYS DO IT AGAIN.

WHERE ARE YOU?
I'M IN HERE.

WHAT IF WE STOPPED THIS CYCLE?
THERE'S SOMETHING BEHIND THE BACKBOARD OF THIS DRAWER.
IT'S BEEN WAITING A LONG TIME FOR SUCH AN OCCASION.
OUTSIDE THE GUEST ROOM.
NUK NUK NUK
HELLO, IT'S THE HOTEL MANAGER, HELEN.
ARE YOU ALRIGHT IN THERE?
SHE'S GOING TO TRY AND STOP YOU. I'D DO IT NOW.

SEBASTIAN'S ROOM.
GUESS I WON'T BE NEEDING THIS ANYMORE.

UH! DIDN'T SEE YOU THERE. OR DID YOU JUST APPEAR?
UM, CAN I... HELP YOU?

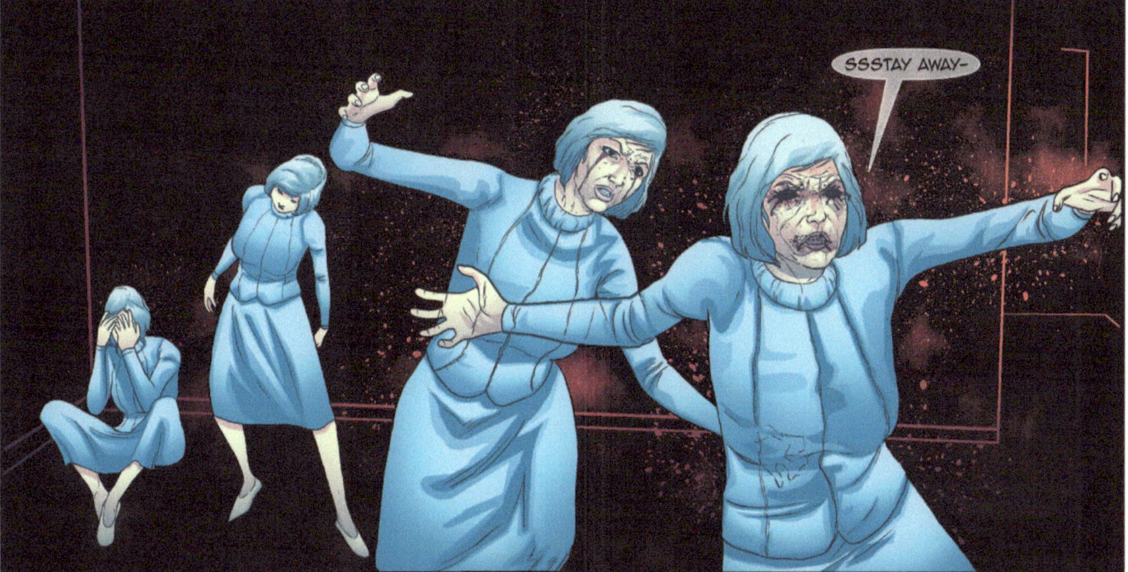

SSSTAY AWAY—

—FROM MY CLAIRE!

WHOA!
WHAT THE HELL JUST HAPPENED?!

HOTEL LOBBY.
HELEN? OH.

The Avira takes another victim.

SORRY SEBASTIAN, WE HAD A FATALITY AND I HAVE TO SORT OUT A CLEANER.
BUT I CAN CATCH UP WITH YOU AT DINNERTIME.

OKAY, I'M SORRY TO HEAR ABOUT THE DEATH. I'LL SEE YOU LATER.

There are ghosts everywhere!
Wait a minute, the freak elevator accident of 1957. I studied this case.
Three pairs of twins died simultaneously in the fall.

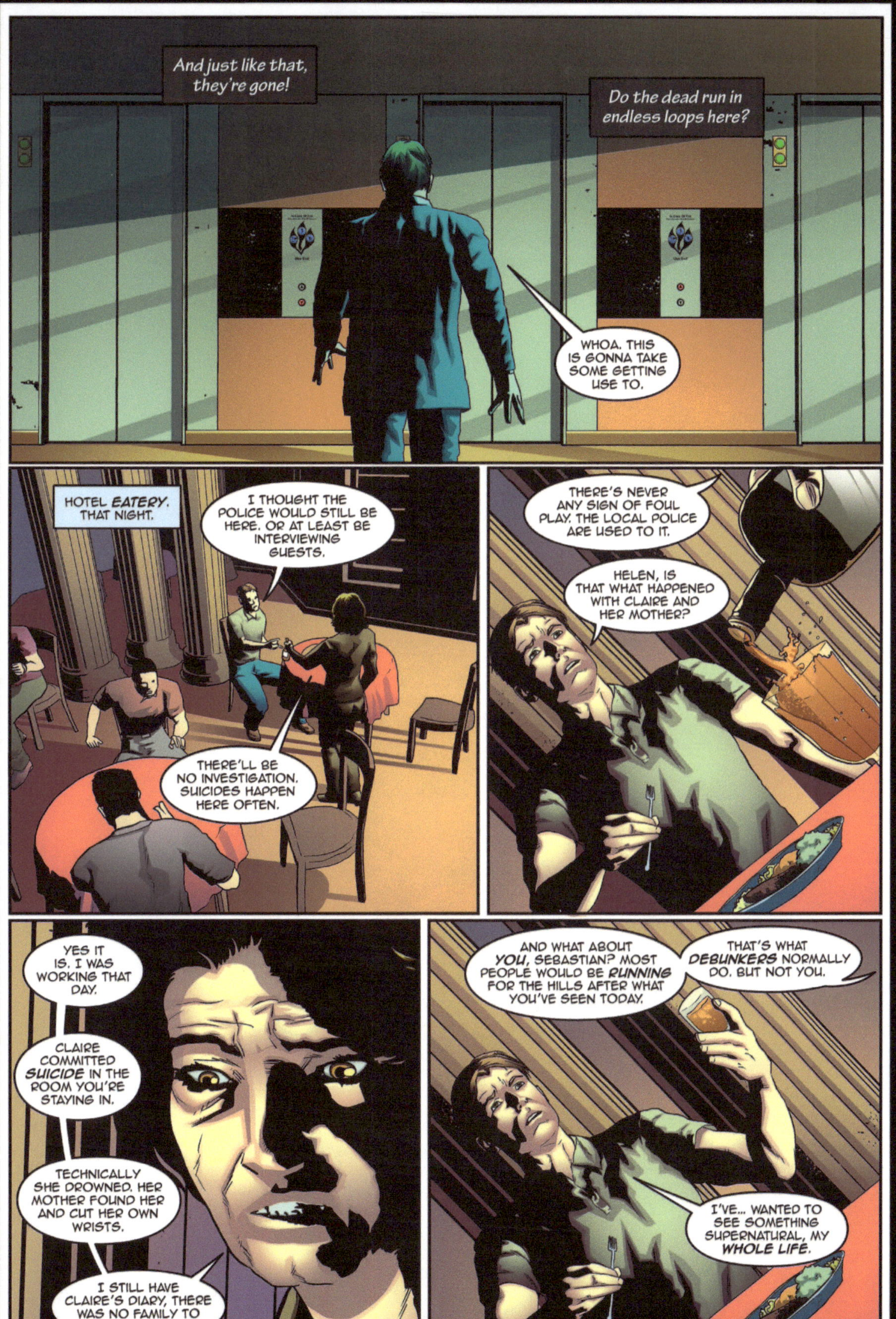

And just like that, they're gone!
Do the dead run in endless loops here?
WHOA. THIS IS GONNA TAKE SOME GETTING USE TO.
HOTEL EATERY. THAT NIGHT.
I THOUGHT THE POLICE WOULD STILL BE HERE. OR AT LEAST BE INTERVIEWING GUESTS.
THERE'LL BE NO INVESTIGATION. SUICIDES HAPPEN HERE OFTEN.
THERE'S NEVER ANY SIGN OF FOUL PLAY. THE LOCAL POLICE ARE USED TO IT.
HELEN, IS THAT WHAT HAPPENED WITH CLAIRE AND HER MOTHER?
YES IT IS. I WAS WORKING THAT DAY.
CLAIRE COMMITTED SUICIDE IN THE ROOM YOU'RE STAYING IN.
TECHNICALLY SHE DROWNED. HER MOTHER FOUND HER AND CUT HER OWN WRISTS.
I STILL HAVE CLAIRE'S DIARY, THERE WAS NO FAMILY TO CLAIM IT.
AND WHAT ABOUT YOU, SEBASTIAN? MOST PEOPLE WOULD BE RUNNING FOR THE HILLS AFTER WHAT YOU'VE SEEN TODAY.
THAT'S WHAT DEBUNKERS NORMALLY DO. BUT NOT YOU.
I'VE... WANTED TO SEE SOMETHING SUPERNATURAL, MY WHOLE LIFE.

SEBASTIAN, LET ME SHOW YOU SOMETHING.
MY FAMILY BUILT THE HOTEL AVIRA. MANY OF THEM WERE BORN HERE.
AND JUST AS THIS PLACE HAS A HISTORY OF DARKNESS, THERE'S ALSO A MIRACULOUS SIDE.
A PROFITABLE SIDE.
RECEPTION OFFICE.

THERE WAS A TRIBE OF ABORIGINALS WHO LIVED ON THIS LAND.
NOT MUCH IS KNOWN ABOUT THEM, BUT THE TOWN LEGEND SAYS A SPIRIT WATCHED OVER THEM.
SOMETIMES I WONDER IF THAT SPIRIT WATCHES OVER THE AVIRA.

THIS HOTEL WAS THE FOUNDING BLOCK OF WHAT BECAME MY FAMILY'S WEALTH.
IN FACT, IT STILL TURNS OVER A SUBSTANTIAL REVENUE, THANKS TO ITS REPUTATION AS A HAUNTED LOCATION.
TAX, POLICE, LAW, EVERYTHING HAS EVENTUALLY GIVEN WAY TO THE HOTEL'S BEST INTEREST.
AND THE FEW DEBUNKERS WHO HAVE STAYED HERE, NEVER RETURN.

THE INDOOR PLANTS HERE ALL THRIVE, YET REQUIRE VIRTUALLY NO MAINTENANCE.
THE BUILDING ITSELF HAS RARELY SHOWN SIGNS OF DECAY IN ITS ENTIRE HISTORY.
BUT THE ABUNDANCE COMES WITH A PRICE. SO I'LL WARN YOU A SECOND TIME.

BE CAREFUL WITH THE GHOSTS HERE: IT'S YOUR ATTENTION ON THEM THAT MAKES THEM SEEM REAL.

SEBASTIAN'S ROOM: BATHROOM. LATER THAT NIGHT.
CLAIRE! YOU'RE BACK! I'VE BEEN LOOKING FOR YOU.

SEBASTIAN...
YOU CAN TOUCH ME?

WHY WOULDN'T I BE ABLE TO?
DO YOU WANT ME TO LEAVE?

NO. I HAVEN'T FELT THIS ALIVE FOR YEARS.

STAY WITH ME, CLAIRE.

I WANT YOU.

MAKE LOVE TO ME SEBASTIAN.

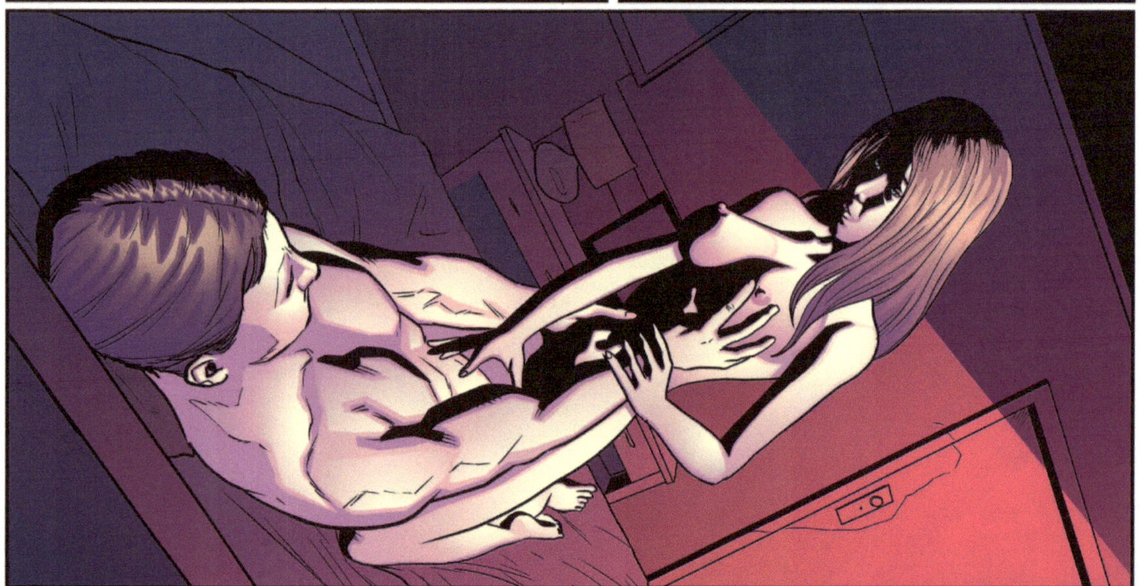

THE HOTEL AVIRA LOBBY.
What the hell?

I was just with Claire.. and then...
What's happened to the Lobby?

January 1970
Sun Mon Tue Wed Thu Fri Sat
1 2 3
4 5 6 7 8 9 10
11 12 13 14 15 16 17
18 19 20 21 22 23 24
25 26 27 28 29 30 31
April 1970
Sun Mon Tue Wed Thu Fri Sat
1 2 3 4
5 6 7 8 9 10 11
12 13 14 15 16 17 18
19 20 21 22 23 24 25
26 27 28 29 30
July 1970
Sun Mon Tue Wed Thu Fri Sat
1 2 3 4
5 6 7 8 9 10 11
12 13 14 15 16 17 18
19 20 21 22 23 24 25
26 27 28 29 30 31
February 1970
Sun Mon Tue Wed Thu Fri Sat
1 2 3 4 5 6 7
8 9 10 11 12 13 14
15 16 17 18 19 20 21
22 23 24 25 26 27 28
May 1970
Sun Mon Tue Wed Thu Fri Sat
1 2
3 4 5 6 7
10 11 12 13
17 18 19 20
24 25 26 27
31
August
Sun Mon Tue
2 3 4
9 10 11
March 1970
Sun Mon Tue Wed Thu Fri Sat
1 2 3 4 5 6 7
8 9 10 11 12 13 14
15 16 17 18 19 20 21
22 23 24 25 26 27 28

OH, NO.
NO!
NO!

THE HOTEL AVIRA HAUNTINGS #2

CHAPTER 2: CLAIRE

THE YEAR 1970. THE HOTEL AVIRA.
This can't be happening.
It's a hallucination of some sort.
No lift, again.
HELLO?
IT'S TIME, SEBASTIAN.
FUCK NO!

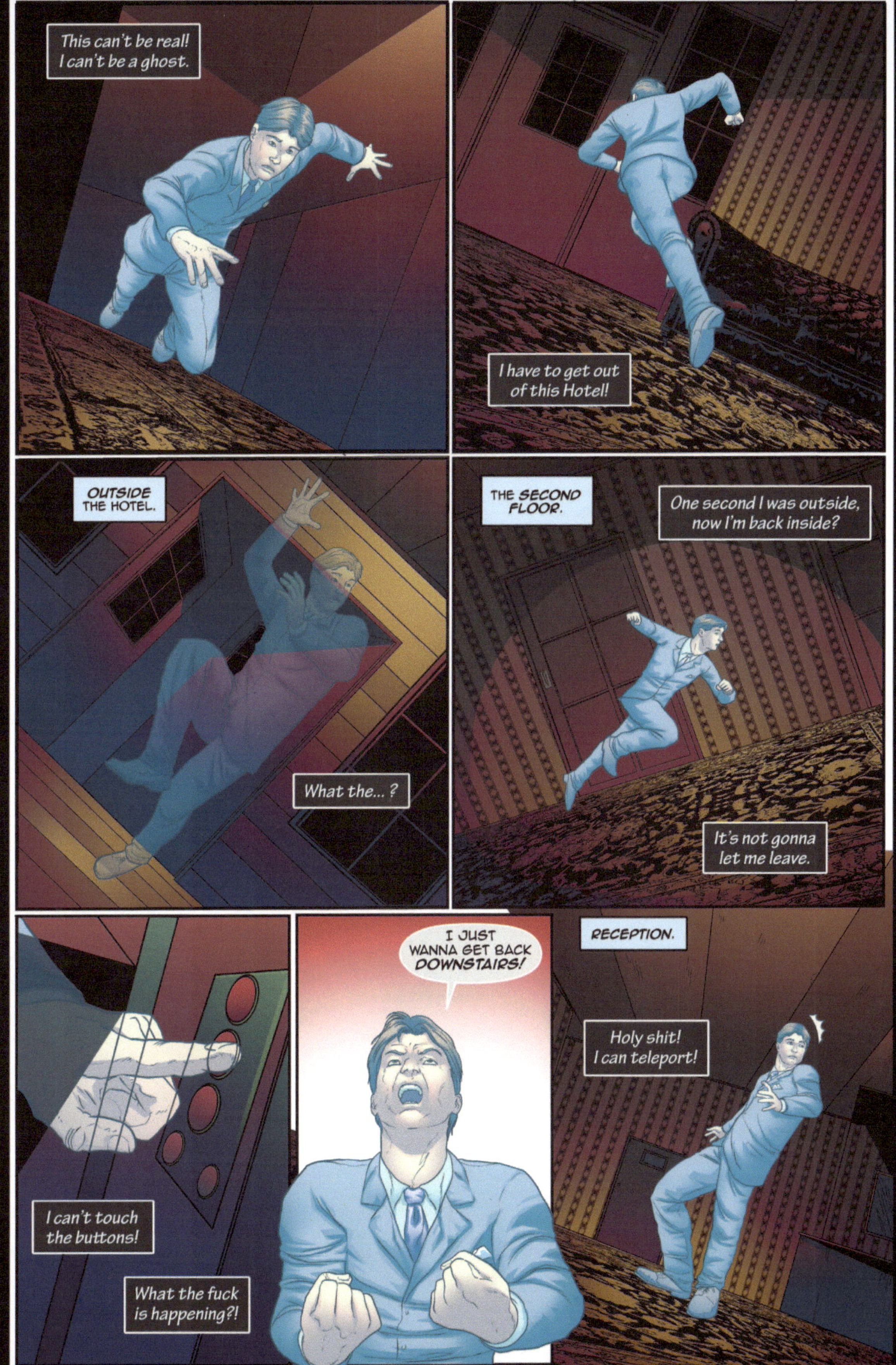
This can't be real!
I can't be a ghost.

I have to get out
of this Hotel!

OUTSIDE THE HOTEL.

What the... ?

THE SECOND FLOOR.

One second I was outside,
now I'm back inside?

It's not gonna
let me leave.

I JUST WANNA GET BACK
DOWNSTAIRS!

RECEPTION.

Holy shit!
I can teleport!

I can't touch
the buttons!

What the fuck
is happening?!

EXCUSE ME! THE DATE. IS IT 1970?

YES IT IS, SIR. MY NAME IS HELEN.
DID YOU HAVE A RESERVATION WITH US?

OH!
RESERVATION FOR MR TUCKER AND FAMILY THANK YOU!

AHH.. UM...

ARE YOU A GHOST?
WHAT? NO. YES, I MEAN, AT THIS POINT IN TIME, YES.

GIRL! GIRL! DO YOU HAVE OUR RESERVATION?
UM, YES. SORRY, SIR. I'M NEW AT THIS.
THE TUCKER FAMILY ISN'T IT?
SNAP
There's got to be a way back to my time, to my body.
Claire! She's still alive here.
SLOW DOWN, CLAIRE! I'M NOT THAT FAST THESE DAYS.
OKAY MOTHER. I'LL TAKE YOU TO RECEPTION THEN COLLECT OUR LUGGAGE.
GOOD DAY.
She can see me. But doesn't know me.
AH, GOOD DAY.
Maybe there's a purpose for me being here.
Maybe I've got something to do before I go back.

If Claire can see me, then she can probably hear me.
What if I wait until she's settled in?

NIGHT.
Nighttime. How'd that happen? Hours have passed in an instant.
So why'd I wake up now?

EATERY.

HI THERE, I'M SEBASTIAN. MIND IF I JOIN YOU?
ACTUALLY, SOME COMPANY SOUNDS GOOD. I'M CLAIRE.

RECEPTION.
BUT THERE'S ACTUAL GHOSTS HERE! I'M LOOKING AT ONE RIGHT NOW!
YOU TOLD ME, BUT I DIDN'T THINK YOU MEANT IT.

NO! YOU'VE GOT TO GET SOMEONE TO REPLACE ME!
THREE DAYS? I CAN'T SLEEP HERE WITH GHOSTS RUNNING AROUND!
ACTUALLY, I'M STUDYING TO BECOME A VET. OR ASSISTANT VET.
I'VE TAKEN SOME TIME OFF TO LOOK AFTER MY MOTHER. SHE'S NOT WELL THESE DAYS
MAKES SENSE, BUT WHY THIS HOTEL?
I feel different around her.
Claire's ghost became more physical when we interacted.
YOU JOKING? THE HOTEL AVIRA IS AN ICON! EVERYONE HAS TO DO IT AT LEAST ONCE.
THEY SAY YOU CAN SEE GHOSTS HERE!
Can I touch her?
CLAIRE, LISTEN TO ME. YOU ONLY HAVE ONE LIFE TO LIVE.
Yes.
YOU'RE VERY FORWARD! I'VE ONLY JUST MET YOU.
THAT'S NOT WHAT I MEANT!

YOU TOUCHED HER.
YEAH, STILL TRYING TO FIGURE THAT ONE OUT MYSELF. ANYWAY, I'M SEBASTIAN.
MIKE, WHAT YEAR DID YOU DIE IN?
ACTUALLY, I'M FROM THE FUTURE. SOMEHOW MY SPIRIT GOT TRAPPED IN THE PAST.
PROVE IT.
THIS IS WHAT A PHONE LOOKS LIKE WHERE I COME FROM. THIS ONE DOESN'T WORK.
LIKE MY SUIT, IT SEEMS TO BE A BEST-CASE SCENARIO REPRESENTATION OF THINGS I GENERALLY HAVE ON ME.
IT LOOKS LIKE A STAR TREK COMMUNICATOR.
IT DOES.
MIKE, WOULD YOU GET A MESSAGE TO THAT GOOD-LOOKING WOMAN I WAS TALKING WITH?

THE SECOND FLOOR.
CLAIRE IS RESTING YOUNG MAN.
NOW PLEASE GO AND BOTHER SOMEONE ELSE!
BUT I PROMISED I'D GET A MESSAGE TO HER!

CHILDREN, NO RESPECT FOR THEIR ELDERS THESE DAYS.
IT'S ALRIGHT, MOTHER.

HOW CAN I HELP YOU?
DOES HE REALLY?
I'M MIKE. MY FRIEND SEBASTIAN SAYS HE'S SORRY FOR SCARING YOU.
HE WANTS TO SEE YOU AGAIN FOR DINNER TOMORROW NIGHT.

TELL HIM 'MAYBE'. GOODNIGHT, MIKE.

Dear Diary, today I met a strange man called, Sebastian.
No, not strange. He is VERY strange.

MORNING.
CLAIRE!
SEBASTIAN! SHAME ON YOU! ASKING A CHILD TO SET UP YOUR DATES.
WELL YEAH, IT'S COWARDLY OF ME.
BUT YOU SEEMED THREATENED BY GROWN MEN.
OH MY GOD!
I CAN'T BELIEVE YOU JUST SAID THAT!
SEBASTIAN!
DON'T YOU START WITH ME, BOY!
BUT THERE HE IS!
'MORNING MIKE!
THAT MAN'S ALWAYS ANGRY.
ANYWAY, YOU WANT TO ACCOMPANY ME TO THE SHOPS?
I DON'T THINK THAT'S A GOOD IDEA.
OH! OKAY.
DON'T GET ME WRONG, I'D LIKE TO.
YOU'RE A STRANGE MAN, SEBASTIAN.
SEE YOU TONIGHT.
THERE ARE JUST SOME THINGS I NEED TO SORT OUT HERE BEFORE I CAN MOVE ON.
SEE YOU TONIGHT?

MOMENTS LATER.
HELLO, DEAR. I'M EXPECTING A DELIVERY TO HELP WITH MY SLEEP.
Helen said Claire dies from sleeping pills!*
* SEE SLEEPING WITH GHOSTS 1.

THERE WE ARE, MRS CLARKSON. ARRIVED FIRST THING THIS MORNING.

HELEN, YOU'VE GOT TO HELP ME.
HER DAUGHTER, CLAIRE, IS GOING TO KILL HERSELF WITH THOSE PILLS!
YOU'RE NOT REAL. YOU'RE JUST A GHOST!

THE SECOND FLOOR.
PLEASE! IF YOU CAN HEAR ME, OR SENSE ME, YOU NEED TO THROW AWAY THOSE PILLS!
CLAIRE'S LIFE DEPENDS ON IT!
No reaction, I'm invisible to her.

Well, if no one else will help me, maybe you can.
WHY'D YOU BRING ME TO THE PAST? IF I CAN'T CHANGE ANYTHING, WHAT'S THE POINT?
YOU BROUGHT YOURSELF HERE.
THIS IS WHAT YOU WANTED TO SEE: LIFE AFTER DEATH.
TAKE MY HAND, FORGET YOUR OLD LIFE. LIVE HERE ETERNAL.
WHY THE HELL WOULD I WANT THAT?
SOON CLAIRE WILL BE DEAD, AND YOU CAN SHARE FOREVER WITH HER.

I WANT TO SAVE HER! NOT LET HER COMMIT SUICIDE!

NO. YOU CAME HERE TO SUCCUMB, SEBASTIAN FLETCHER.
HEY! BACK UP!

YOU ARE THE MAN WHO MARRIED A WOMAN HE DIDN'T LOVE.
TOOK A JOB HE DIDN'T WANT.
I WANT TO BE IN THE LOBBY NOW!

LOBBY.
SHIT!
LIVED A LIFE DICTATED BY THE LOWEST COMMON DENOMINATOR.
AND WHEN HE FINALLY GOT THROUGH HIS DIVORCE, EXPLORED THE DARK PLEASURES OF LIFE.
I want to be on the second floor NOW!

CLAIRE AND MOTHER'S ROOM.
SLEPT WITH PROSTITUTES, TRIED ILLEGAL DRUGS.
FOR FUCK'S SAKE!
SEARCHED FOR SOMETHING MORE THAN WHAT THE PHYSICAL WORLD COULD OFFER.

STOP! I DON'T WANT THIS ANYMORE!
AND WHEN YOU FELT NOTHING FROM CHEAP TRICKS, YOU SOUGHT OUT THE SUPERNATURAL.

ANYTHING TO GET YOU AWAY FROM THE MUNDANE EXISTENCE OF LIFE.
WHAT ARE YOU?!

I AM THE HATE THAT BURNS BELOW THE SURFACE.
THE WOUND THAT KEEPS BLEEDING.
I AM UNTOLD HISTORY.
I want to be AWAY from this fucking thing!

LOBBY.
The Lobby again. But somehow it's nighttime.
Another time slip? Something important must be about to happen.

Why am I puffed?
I don't breath air.

CLAIRE AND MOTHER'S ROOM.

I DON'T THINK IT'S A VERY GOOD IDEA YOU HAVING DINNER WITH SOME MAN YOU ONLY JUST MET.

I DON'T WANT TO GO THROUGH THIS AGAIN MOTHER! I'LL BE BACK IN A FEW HOURS.

MOMENTS LATER.

Who is this man?

What do I do if Claire leaves me?

LOBBY.

GOOD EVENING.

I've seen that dress before. Her ghost wears it.

This is the night Claire dies!

EATERY.
I FEEL STRANGE EATING IN FRONT OF YOU. SURE YOU DON'T WANT SOME OF MINE?
NO, THANK YOU. BUT THERE'S SOMETHING I REALLY NEED TO TALK TO YOU ABOUT.

SO YOU DID MEET HIM FOR DINNER!

WHAK
WHAK
WHAK
MICHAEL TUCKER!
HOW MANY TIMES DO I HAVE TO TELL YOU TO STOP TELLING FIBS!
OW!
BUT HE'S RIGHT THERE!

IT'S OKAY, HE WASN'T BOTHERING US.
YOUR SON SET THIS DATE UP.

THAT CHAIR'S EMPTY!
STOP ENCOURAGING HIM.

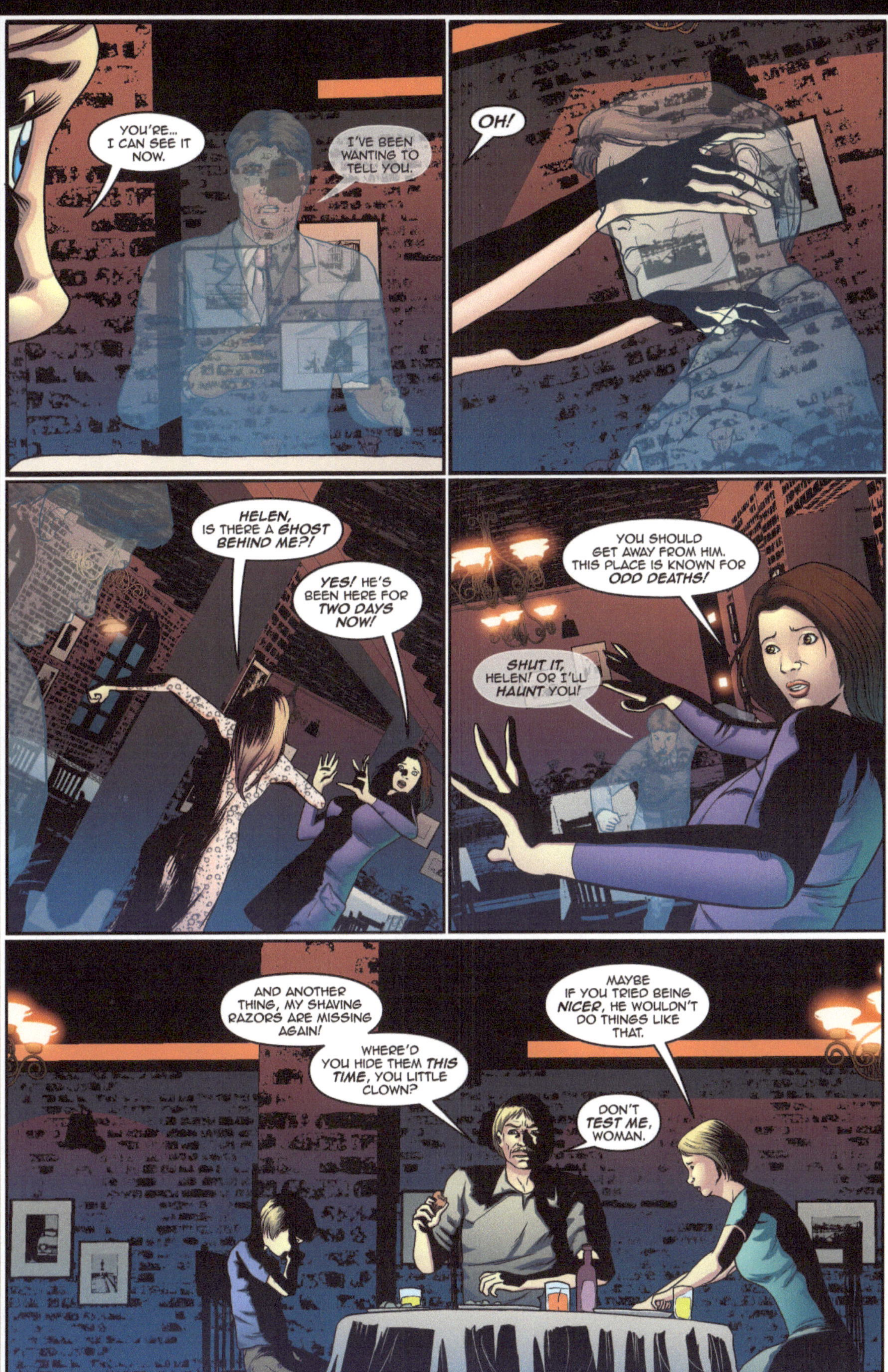

YOU'RE... I CAN SEE IT NOW.
I'VE BEEN WANTING TO TELL YOU.
OH!
HELEN, IS THERE A GHOST BEHIND ME?!
YES! HE'S BEEN HERE FOR TWO DAYS NOW!
YOU SHOULD GET AWAY FROM HIM. THIS PLACE IS KNOWN FOR ODD DEATHS!
SHUT IT, HELEN! OR I'LL HAUNT YOU!
AND ANOTHER THING, MY SHAVING RAZORS ARE MISSING AGAIN!
WHERE'D YOU HIDE THEM THIS TIME, YOU LITTLE CLOWN?
MAYBE IF YOU TRIED BEING NICER, HE WOULDN'T DO THINGS LIKE THAT.
DON'T TEST ME, WOMAN.

CLAIRE AND MOTHER'S ROOM.
I DON'T WANT TO DISCUSS IT, MOTHER.
WE'RE LEAVING TONIGHT!

CLAIRE, YOU'RE BEING IRRATIONAL! I CAN'T JUST PACK UP AND LEAVE TONIGHT, MY HEART WOULDN'T TAKE IT.

DAMN IT! FIRST THING TOMORROW THEN!

FINE!

SECOND FLOOR CORRIDOR.

HELLO, ROOM SERVICE? YES, THIS IS MRS CLARKSON.
I'D LIKE TO ORDER A HOT CHOCOLATE PLEASE.
RECEPTION.
LISTEN TO ME, THAT WOMAN, CLAIRE? IF WE DON'T DO SOMETHING, SHE'LL OVERDOSE ON THOSE SLEEPING PILLS THAT CAME IN TODAY.
NO, YOU'RE TRYING TO TRICK ME.
I'M REALLY NOT. THERE'S A DEMON IN THIS HOTEL. IT COLLECTS THE SOULS OF PEOPLE WHO DIE HERE.
PLEASE HELP ME SAVE CLAIRE.
THERE'S NO DEMON HERE. JUST YOU, TRYING TO MAKE ME LOSE MY MIND.
BUT YOU'RE NOT GOING TO GET ME!
THE DEMON LIVES IN THE HOTEL ELEVATOR SHAFT.
CLAIRE WILL OVERDOSE ON SLEEPING PILLS, FALL ASLEEP IN THE BATH AND DROWN.
THEN THE DEMON WILL CLAIM HER SOUL.

I'VE RUN YOU A HOT BATH.
YOU ALWAYS LIKED A GOOD SOAK WHEN YOU WERE UPSET.
SECOND FLOOR CORRIDOR.

I HAVE TO GO BACK TO MY LIFE, MOTHER. I NEED TO FINISH MY STUDIES.
I KNOW, DEAR. I'LL JUST HAVE TO GET USED TO THE IDEA OF LETTING YOU GO.

YOU JUST RELAX TONIGHT.
WE CAN GET ROOM SERVICE FOR DINNER LATER ON.

I LOVE YOU, MOTHER.
I LOVE YOU TOO, DEAR. MORE THAN ANYTHING IN THE WORLD.

OUTSIDE THE HOTEL ENTRY.
YOU'RE NOT GOING TO FOLLOW ME?
I CAN'T! THE DEMON TRAPS US HERE.
I STEP OUT THERE, I APPEAR BACK IN THE HOTEL SOMEWHERE.
HOW DO I KNOW YOU'RE TELLING ME THE TRUTH?
HELEN, WE DON'T HAVE TIME FOR THIS!
JUST MEET ME UPSTAIRS!
Claire's room, NOW!
CLAIRE AND MOTHER'S ROOM.
I'M SORRY, CLAIRE.

CLAIRE?

CAN YOU HEAR ME?

OH, NO.

CLAIRE WAKE UP!
YOUR MOTHER'S GOING TO DROWN YOU!

CHAPTER 3: HELEN

THE YEAR 1970. THE HOTEL AVIRA.
YOU HAVE TO HELP ME, HELEN!
CLAIRE IS UPSTAIRS RIGHT NOW, LYING IN A BATHTUB PASSED OUT.
IF WE DON'T DO SOMETHING, HER MOTHER IS GOING TO DROWN HER.
JUST LEAVE ME ALONE. PLEASE!
YOU'RE TRYING TO MAKE ME LOSE MY MIND!
IF SHE DIES TONIGHT, IT'S YOUR FAULT, HELEN!
IT IS TIME, SEBASTIAN.
I'M READY!
TAKE MY HAND. EXIST HERE ETERNAL.
I DON'T THINK SO.

AAAARRG!
YOU'LL HELP ME OR I'LL TEAR YOU APART!

HOTEL AVIRA. THE PRESENT.
SEBASTIAN'S ROOM.
UH!
I'm back!

Guess it didn't like me interfering with history.
CLAIRE? ARE YOU STILL HERE?

SSSTAY AWAY!
FOR FUCK'S SAKE!
The more things change-

GROUND FLOOR.
-The more they stay the same.

YOU KNOW, HE LOOKS FAMILIAR.
MICHAEL TUCKER, YOU THINK EVERYONE LOOKS FAMILIAR.

HELEN, I NEED TO SEE CLAIRE'S DIARY.
YOU WOULDN'T BELIEVE WHERE I'VE JUST BEEN!
RECEPTION.
EXIT

RECEPTION OFFICE.
THERE IT IS, THE ENTRY ABOUT MEETING ME!

SEBASTIAN, I FEEL.. STRANGE.
I'VE GOT YOU!

THE YEAR 1970.
HELLO? SEBASTIAN, ARE YOU STILL IN THERE?

WHERE'S THE LIFT... THIS CANNOT BE REAL.

WHO'S PLAYING WITH THE LIGHTS!?

LANDOWNER.
W-WHO'S THERE?

OH, LET ME OUT! LET ME OUT!

WHAT'S GOING ON? WHERE'S THE LOCK?!
HELP ME! SOMEBODY HELP ME!
OH MY GOD, AM I DEAD?
G...G...GHOSTS!

OH NO!
I'M ALIVE, I'M STILL ALIVE. THIS ISN'T REAL!
LANDOWNER, WHAT ARE YOU DOING IN MY REALM?
PLEASE, PLEASE, PLEASE, GET ME OUT OF HERE!
MIKE! MIKE, THERE ARE GHOSTS HERE! I MEAN REAL GHOSTS! A LOT OF THEM!
I KNOW! I KEEP TELLING MY MUM AND DAD. AND THEY THINK I'M FIBBING.
YOU OKAY, LADY?

THE PRESENT.
ARE YOU SURE YOU DON'T WANT TO SIT DOWN?

NO. THANK YOU. I'M ALRIGHT NOW.
MY ARM FEELS ITCHY, THOUGH. I'VE NEVER SEEN THIS SCAR BEFORE.

AND.. I REMEMBER MEETING YOU WHEN I JUST STARTED WORKING HERE.
I MAY HAVE CHANGED SOMETHING IN THE PAST
WHICH MEANS IF THE PRESENT CAN BE ALTERED, I CAN STILL SAVE CLAIRE.
BUT I NEED SOMETHING FROM YOU: HELP ME EARN THE TRUST OF YOUR EARLIER SELF.

YOU'D GO BACK?
I CAN STILL FEEL THE PATH.
AND I HAVE AN IDEA OF HOW TO JOLT MYSELF BACK THERE.

AND WHAT IF YOU GET TRAPPED?
YOUR SPIRIT THERE, YOUR BODY HERE?
I CAN'T FOCUS ON THAT NOW.

SOON AFTER.
THE LOBBY LIFTS.
SEBASTIAN, ARE YOU LOOKING FOR ME?
IN A WAY.
LET'S GO SEE YOUR MOTHER.
THE SECOND FLOOR.
CLAIRE, STAY BEHIND ME.
YOOOU!
GAH!

1970.
JUST KEEP YOUR DISTANCE, DEAD MAN.
SO, I'VE BEEN IN THE ELEVATOR SHAFT.
THERE'S A DEMON IN THERE THAT COLLECTS SOULS.
I THINK IT KNOWS MY FAMILY.
YES, IT DOES.
HELEN, I'M GOING TO TELL YOU A STORY ABOUT A LITTLE GIRL WHO FELL IN LOVE WITH A BOY WHO LIVED ACROSS THE ROAD.
THE GIRL'S FAMILY HAD TO MOVE FOR WORK. THEY WERE GOING TO TAKE OVER RUNNING A FAMILY BUSINESS, A HOTEL.
THE GIRL ALWAYS WANTED TO KISS THE BOY BUT WAS AFRAID TO.
ON THE DAY OF THE MOVE, SHE WANTED TO SEE THE BOY ONE LAST TIME, BUT HER PARENTS WOULDN'T LET HER GO.
THEY DIDN'T BELIEVE A GIRL HER AGE COULD FEEL LOVE.
AND I'VE ALWAYS REGRETTED NOT RUNNING OVER TO CHARLIE'S HOUSE AND KISSING HIM GOODBYE.

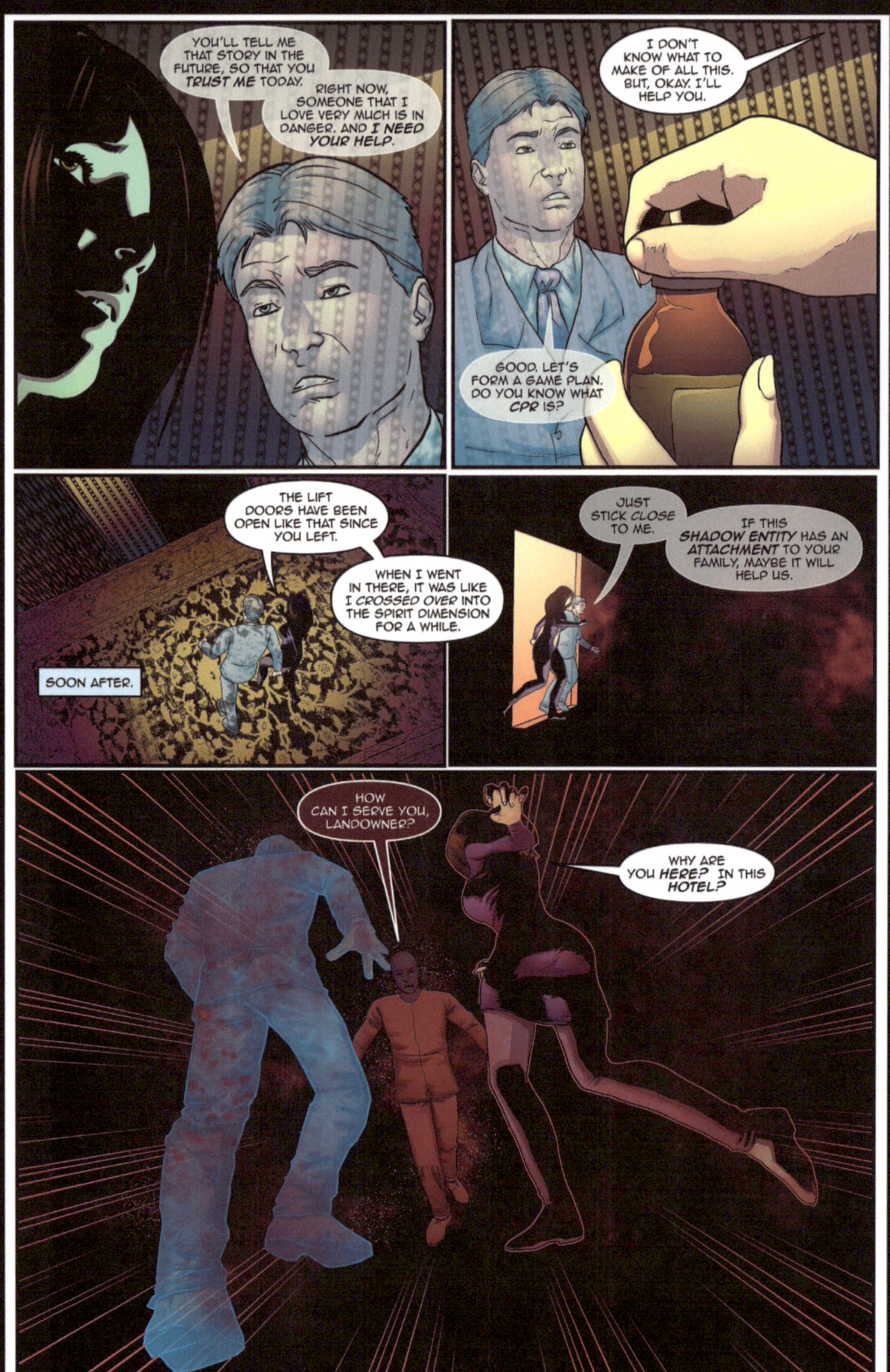

YOU'LL TELL ME THAT STORY IN THE FUTURE, SO THAT YOU TRUST ME TODAY.
RIGHT NOW, SOMEONE THAT I LOVE VERY MUCH IS IN DANGER. AND I NEED YOUR HELP.
I DON'T KNOW WHAT TO MAKE OF ALL THIS. BUT, OKAY, I'LL HELP YOU.
GOOD, LET'S FORM A GAME PLAN. DO YOU KNOW WHAT CPR IS?
THE LIFT DOORS HAVE BEEN OPEN LIKE THAT SINCE YOU LEFT.
WHEN I WENT IN THERE, IT WAS LIKE I CROSSED OVER INTO THE SPIRIT DIMENSION FOR A WHILE.
SOON AFTER.
JUST STICK CLOSE TO ME.
IF THIS SHADOW ENTITY HAS AN ATTACHMENT TO YOUR FAMILY, MAYBE IT WILL HELP US.
HOW CAN I SERVE YOU, LANDOWNER?
WHY ARE YOU HERE? IN THIS HOTEL?

THESE WERE MY PEOPLE. I WAS THEIR LAND SPIRIT.
SEBASTIAN! WHAT'S HAPPENED?
IT'S OKAY, HELEN. I CAN SEE IT TOO. IT'S LIKE WE'VE MOVED INTO A HOLOGRAM OF THE PAST!
YOUR KIND INVADED THE LAND OF MY PEOPLE AND CLAIMED OWNERSHIP OF THE WATER.
AFTER BEING SUBJECTED TO STARVATION, BRUTALIZATION AND MURDER, THE SURVIVING TRIBE MEMBERS ATTACKED A FAMILY THAT HAD MOVED ONTO THEIR LAND.
THIS IS YOUR BLOOD ANCESTOR, LANDOWNER.
SHE ESCAPED THE ATTACK ON HER FAMILY'S HOMESTEAD AND AGAINST THE ODDS, SHE REACHED ANOTHER SETTLEMENT.

THIS WAS THE RETRIBUTION: UNACKNOWLEDGED BUT SANCTIONED MURDER OF THE INDIGENOUS INHABITANTS.

THE ENTIRE TRIBE WAS WIPED OUT.

THEY WERE MY PEOPLE. I STAYED ON THIS LAND, EVEN AFTER IT WAS LEGALLY GIVEN TO YOUR FAMILY.

I ALLOW YOU TO THRIVE, AS I THRIVE ON THE SOULS YOU BRING ME.

COME ON, HELEN. THIS THING WON'T HELP ME.
WE'RE ON OUR OWN.

WE NEED TO GET CLAIRE OUT OF THAT ROOM!

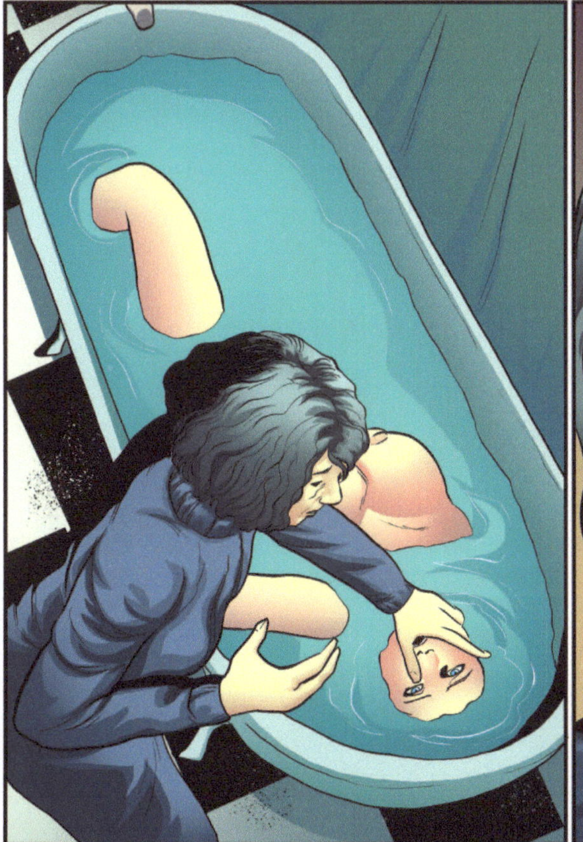

CLAIRE? ARE YOU ASLEEP?
CLAIRE AND MOTHER'S ROOM.

THE SECOND FLOOR.
YEAH, IT DOES THAT.
THE SHADOW LOOKS LIKE YOU NOW!

DON'T LET IT DISTRACT YOU!
CLAIRE'S SOUL IS MINE!

IT ONLY EXISTS HERE BECAUSE OF THE BOND WITH YOUR BLOODLINE!

WHAT ARE YOU DOING?!

GET OUT THIS INSTANT!

I JUST NEED TO CHECK ON YOUR DAUG—
AR-OUH!
CLAIRE WILL DIE. IT IS INEVITABLE.
I'VE HAD ENOUGH OF THIS.
GET OUT OF MY WAY!
AAARRRRGH.

YOU LEAVE THIS INSTANT, OR THERE WILL BE THREE BODIES FOR THE POLICE TO FIND!
THIS CRAZY BITCH JUST CUT ME!
STOP!
GOOD LORD!
TOOK YOU LONG ENOUGH TO SEE ME.
THERE ARE GHOSTS HERE...
THANKS, SEBASTIAN!
CLAIRE!
OH, NO YOU DON'T.

WAKE UP, CLAIRE!
KAH-GAK!
WELCOME BACK!
GET HER AWAY FROM THIS ROOM.
I DON'T WANT TO BE ALONE.

THE BOND YOU HAD WITH MY FAMILY IS OVER. LEAVE THIS PLACE.
AND RELEASE ANY SPIRITS THAT WANT TO LEAVE.

LOBBY.

OUTSIDE THE HOTEL AVIRA.
THE SECOND FLOOR.
SO TIRED.

I MIGHT JUST.. REST HERE...

TWO DAYS LATER.
SEBASTIAN, I'VE COME TO SAY GOODBYE.
YOU LOOK FAMILIAR. DO I KNOW YOU?
CLAIRE.
THANK YOU.

HOTEL AVIRA.
THE PRESENT.
OH MAN.
BACK AGAIN.
WE DID IT.
I THINK.

GOOD MORNING LADIES.

YOU CAN SEE MY MOTHER? I COME HERE ONCE A YEAR TO SPEND SOME TIME WITH HER.

IT'S YOU! ISN'T IT? SEBASTIAN.
IT'S ME. TELL ME HOW YOU'VE BEEN, CLAIRE.

RECEPTION.
AH...
MY NAME IS ELLEN. DID YOU ENJOY YOUR STAY, MR FLETCHER?

I DID. IS THERE A LADY WHO WORKS HERE CALLED HELEN?
THAT WOULD BE MY MOTHER. SHE WORKS IN THE UK NOW, RUNNING THE FAMILY BUSINESS. WE HAVE OFFICES THERE.

I MUST HAVE SEEN HER ON YOUR WEBSITE. INCIDENTALLY, MY STAY HERE WAS LIFE CHANGING.
WE'RE GLAD YOU VISITED. COME AND SEE US AGAIN ANY TIME.

END.

BEHIND THE SCENES OF CHAPTER 1

Art by Marcelo Salaza. Colors by Mike Stefan.

BEHIND THE SCENES OF CHAPTER 2

Art by Marcelo Salaza. Colors by Mike Stefan.

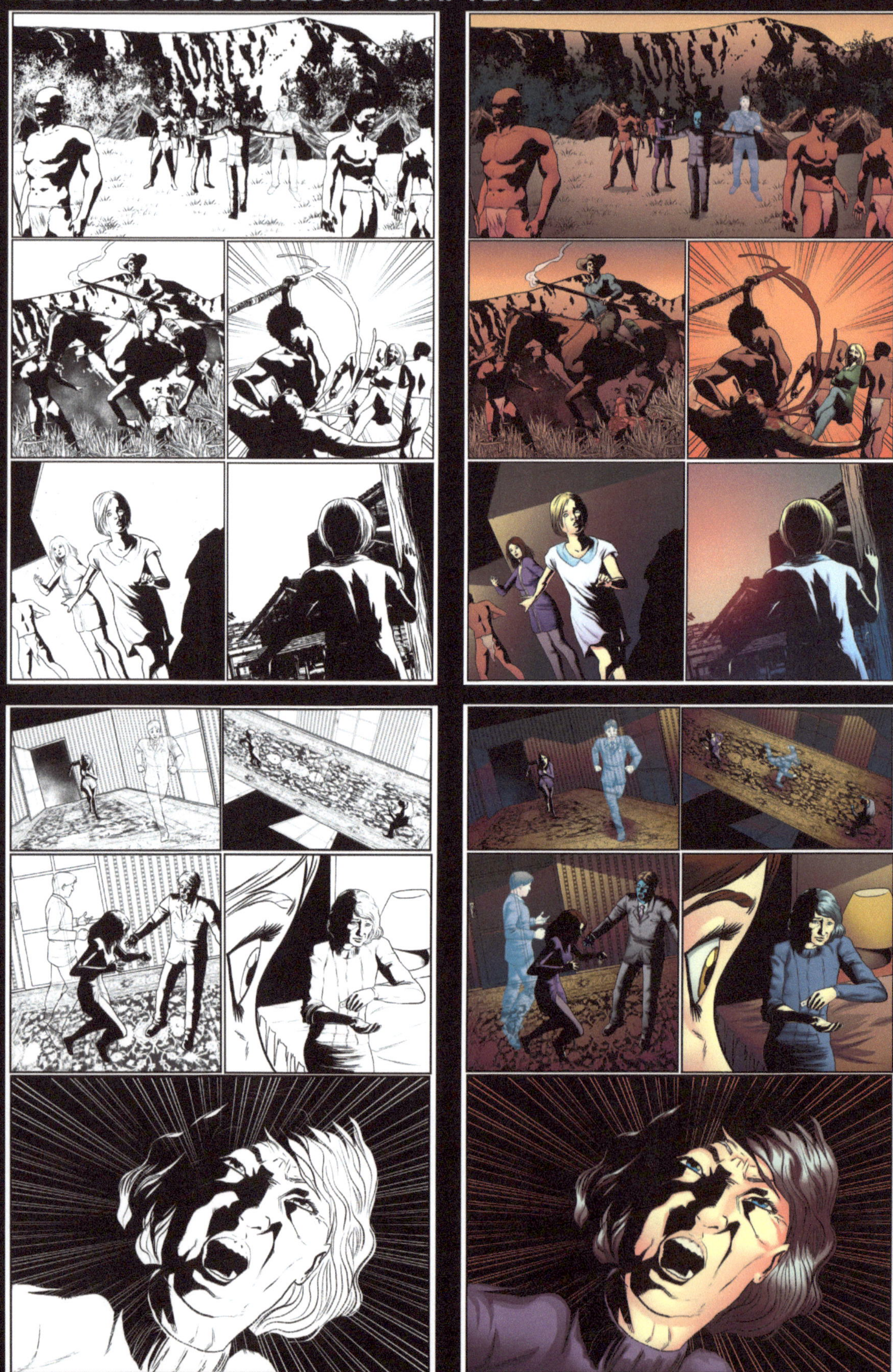

Art by Marcelo Salaza. Colors by Mike Stefan.

SAGE ESCAPE ™
MARS GAMBIT

Print and eBook editions of the graphic novel out now.

ISBN-10: 0994254903
ISBN-13: 978-0994254900

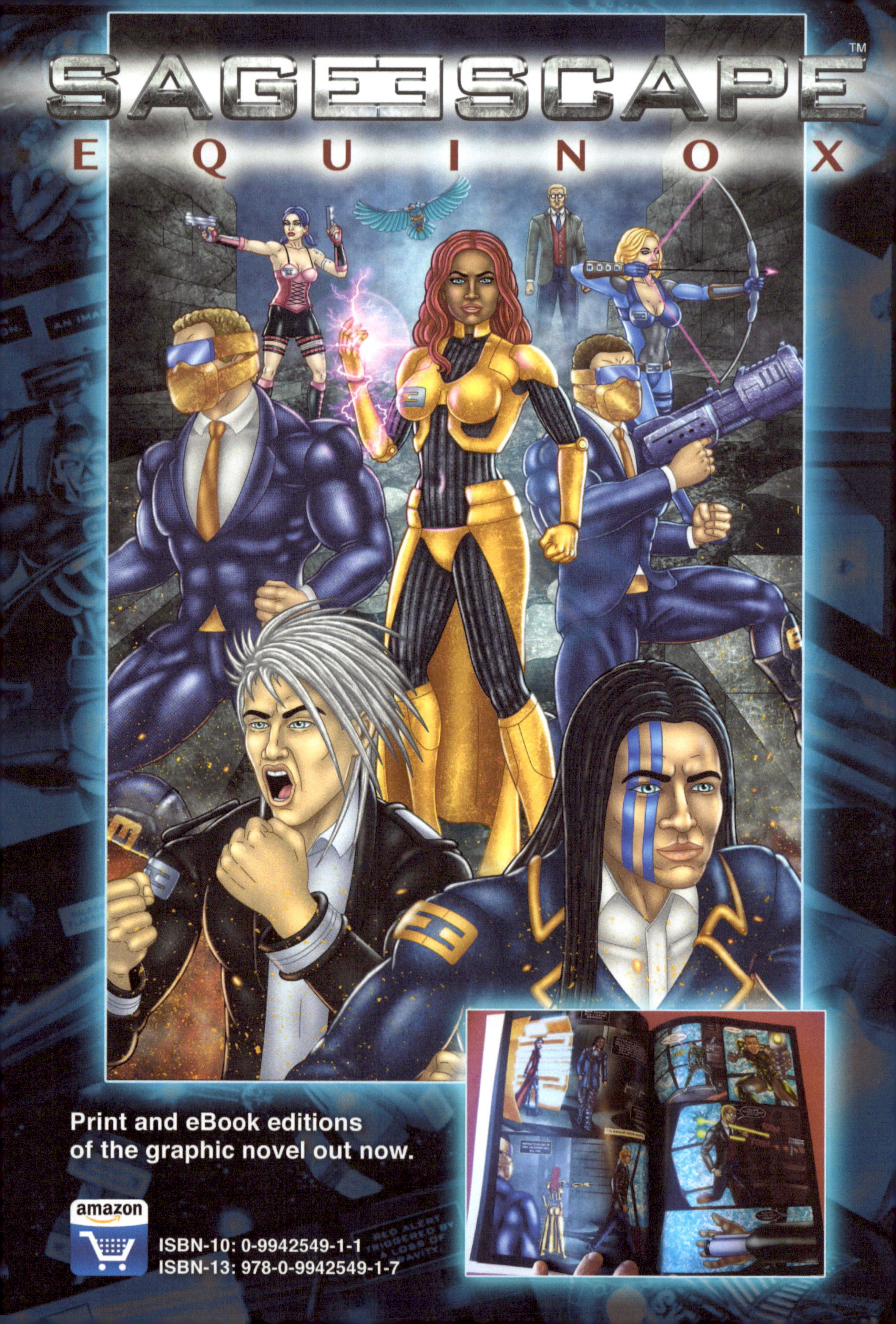

SAGESCAPE™
EQUINOX

Print and eBook editions
of the graphic novel out now.

ISBN-10: 0-9942549-1-1
ISBN-13: 978-0-9942549-1-7

SAGESCAPE
TRANSHUMAN
amazon
ISBN: 978-0994254986
Print and eBook editions of
the graphic novel out now.

RAVAGE
TM
amazon
ISBN-10: 0994254962
ISBN-13: 978-0994254962
Print and eBook editions of
the graphic novel out now.